HORRiD HENRY'S
Cannibal Curse

Francesca Simon spent her childhood on the beach
in California, and then went to Yale and Oxford
Universities to study medieval history and literature.
She now lives in London with her family. She has
written more than 50 books and won the Children's
Book of the Year in 2008 at the Galaxy British Book
Awards for *Horrid Henry and the Abominable Snowman*.

There is a complete list of **Horrid Henry**
titles including picture books, Early Readers, joke
books and gift books at the end of the book.

Visit Horrid Henry's website at
www.horridhenry.co.uk for competitions,
games, downloads and a monthly newsletter!

Also by Francesca Simon

Don't Cook Cinderella
Helping Hercules

and for younger readers

Don't Be Horrid, Henry!
Spider School
The Topsy-Turvies
Do You Speak English, Moon?

HORRiD HENRY'S
Cannibal Curse

Francesca Simon

Illustrated by Tony Ross

Orion
Children's Books

ORION CHILDREN'S BOOKS

First published in Great Britain in 2015 by Orion Children's Books
This edition published in 2016 by Hodder and Stoughton

7 9 10 8 6

Text copyright © Francesca Simon, 2015
Illustrations copyright © Tony Ross, 2015

The moral rights of the author and illustrator have been asserted.

A CIP catalogue record for this book
is available from the British Library.

ISBN 978 1 5101 0227 9

Printed and bound in Great Britain
by Clays Ltd, Elcograf S.p.A.

The paper and board used in this book are
made from wood from responsible sources.

Orion Children's Books
An imprint of
Hachette Children's Group
Part of Hodder and Stoughton
Carmelite House
50 Victoria Embankment
London EC4Y 0DZ

An Hachette UK Company
www.hachette.co.uk

www.hachettechildrens.co.uk
www.horridhenry.co.uk

*For Joshua Stamp-Simon
who has somehow grown up while
Horrid Henry has forever stayed the same*

CONTENTS

HORRiD HENRY'S BAKE-OFF

THWACK!

THWACK!

THWACK!

Moody Margaret thwacked the wall with a stick.

Why oh why did she have to live next door to someone as horrid as Henry?

Her club wasn't safe. Her biscuits weren't safe. And he was such a copy-cat. She'd told everyone she was making a chocolate sponge cake for the street party bake-off competition, and now

Henry was saying he was making a chocolate sponge cake.

And pretending he'd thought of it first.

Well, she'd show him. Her cake was sure to win. For once she'd have the last laugh.

Although . . .

Hmmm . . .

Maybe she could make sure of that . . .

A street party bake-off! Hurrah!

Horrid Henry loved baking. What could be better than choosing exactly what you wanted to eat and then cooking it exactly as you liked it? With loads of extra sugar and lashings of icing?

Horrid Henry loved making fudge. Horrid Henry loved making brownies. Horrid Henry loved baking chocolate cakes.

His parents, unfortunately, only liked him to make horrible food. Pizzas ruined with vegetable toppings. Sloppy gloppy porridge. And if they ever let him make muffins, they had to be wholesome muffins. With wholemeal flour. And bananas. **Ugggh**.

But today, no one could stop him. It was a cake baking contest. And what a cake he'd make. His chocolate sponge cake with extra icing was guaranteed to win. He'd heard that copy-cat Margaret was making one too. Let old frog face try. No one could out-bake Chef Henry.

Plus, the winner would get their picture in the paper, AND be on

3

TV, because the famous
pastry chef Cherry
Berry was coming to
judge.

Whoopee!
Everyone
in Henry's
class was
taking part.
Too
bad, losers,
thought Horrid
Henry, dashing to the
kitchen. Chef Henry is in
the room.

Unfortunately, someone else was too.
Perfect Peter was wearing a Daffy
Daisy apron and peering anxiously at
the oven while Mum took out a baking
tray laden with mysterious grey globs.

'Out of my way, worm,' said Henry.

'I've made cupcakes for the bake-off,' said Peter. 'Look.'

Perfect Peter proudly pointed to the plate covered in lumpy blobs. His name was written on a flag poking out of one cupcake.

'Those aren't cupcakes,' said Henry. 'They're lopsided cowpats.'

'Mum,' wailed Peter. 'Henry called my cupcakes cowpats.'

'Don't be horrid, Henry,' said Mum. 'Peter, I think your cupcakes look— lovely.'

'Plopcakes more like,' said Henry.

'MUM!' screamed Peter. 'Henry said plopcakes.'

'Stop it Henry,' said Mum.

Tee hee.

All the better for him. No need to worry about Peter's saggy disasters winning.

His real competition was Margaret. Henry hated to admit it, but she was almost as good a chef as he was. Well, no way was she beating him today. Her copy-cat chocolate sponge cake wouldn't be a patch on his.

'Henry. Peter. Come out and help hang up the bunting and get cloths on the tables,' said Dad. 'The street party starts at 2 o'clock.'

'But I have to bake my cake,' yelped Henry, weighing the sugar and

6

chocolate. He always put in extra.

'There's plenty of time,' said Mum. 'But I need you to help me now.'

Moody Margaret sneaked through the back door into Henry's kitchen. She'd waited until she'd seen Henry and his family go outside to help set up the tables.

If she was too late and his cake was already baking, she could open the oven door and stomp to make Henry's sponge collapse. Or she could turn the temperature way up high, or scoop out the middle, or—

7

Margaret sniffed.

She couldn't smell anything baking.

What a bit of luck.

There were all Henry's ingredients on the counter, measured out and waiting to be used.

Snatch!

Moody Margaret grabbed the sugar jar and emptied it into the bin. Then she re-filled it with salt.

Tee hee, thought Moody Margaret. Wouldn't it be wonderful to pay Henry back?

'What are you doing here?' came a little voice.

Oops.

Moody Margaret whirled round.

'What are you doing here?' said Margaret.

'I live here,' said Peter.

'I must have come into the wrong house,' said Margaret. 'How silly of me.'

'Out of my way, worm,' came Henry's horrible voice as he slammed the front door.

'Byeeee,' said Margaret, as she skedaddled out of the back door.

Phew.

Revenge was sweet, she thought happily. Or in this case, salty.

Should he tell Henry that Margaret had come over?

No, thought Peter. Henry called my cupcakes plopcakes.

Horrid Henry proudly stuck his name flag in his fabulous cake.

What a triumph.

His glorious chocolate sponge,

9

drowning in luscious icing, was definitely his best ever.

He was sure to win. He was absolutely sure to win. Just wait till Cherry Berry tried a mouthful of his cake. He'd be offered his own TV baking programme. He'd write his own cookbook. But instead of horrible recipes like 10 ways to cook broccoli – as if that would make any difference to how yucky it was – he'd have recipes for things kids actually liked to eat instead of what their parents wanted them to eat.

Chips

Chocolate worms

Frosty Freeze Ice-cream

Veg-free cheese pizza. He'd write: 'Take wrapping off pizza. Put in oven. Or, if you are feeling lazy, ring Pizza Delivery to skip the boring unwrapping and putting in oven bit.'

Yes! He'd add a few recipes with ketchup, then sit back and count the dough.

Horrid Henry sighed happily. Didn't that icing look yummalicious. He'd left loads in the bowl, and more on the spoon. Oh boy, chocolate here I come, thought Horrid Henry. Chefs always taste their own food, don't they, he thought, shoving a huge succulent spoonful into his mouth and—

11

BLECCCCCHHHHHH.
YUCK
AAAARRRRGGGGHH.

Horrid Henry gagged.

Ugh.

He spat it out, gasping and choking.

Ugh.

It tasted worse than anything he'd ever tasted in his life. It was horrible. Disgusting. Revolting. Worse than sprouts.

So bitter. So salty.

Horrid Henry choked down some water.

How was it possible? What could he have done?

He'd been so careful, measuring out the ingredients. How could a teaspoon of salt have got into his icing?

But this wasn't even a teaspoon.

This was a bucket load.

There was only one explanation . . .
Sabotage.

Peter must have done it, in revenge
for Henry calling his cupcakes cowpats.

Wait till I get my hands on you,
Peter, you'll be sorry, you wormy worm
toad—

Wait.

Horrid Henry paused.

Was Perfect Peter evil enough to have
come up with such a dastardly plan?

No.

Was he clever enough?

No.

It had to be someone so vile, so sly, so despicable, they would sabotage a cake.

There was only one person he knew who fitted that description.

Margaret.

Well, he'd show her.

ROOT A TOOT!
ROOT A TOOT!
ROOT A TOOT TOOT TOOT!

Margaret was blasting away on her trumpet. Blasting what she thought was a victory tune.

Not this time, frog face, thought Horrid Henry, sneaking into Moody Margaret's kitchen.

There was her chocolate sponge cake, resting proudly on a flowery china stand. What luck she'd copied him.

Whisk!

Henry snatched Margaret's cake.

14

Switch!

Henry plopped his salt cake on the cake stand instead.

Swap!

He stuck the name flag Margaret into his old cake.

Then he sneaked back home, clutching his stolen one.

Horrid Henry placed his name flag in Margaret's cake and stood back.

He had to admit, Margaret's cake was gorgeous. So chocolatey. So springy. So much chocolate icing whirling and swirling in thick globs.

Margaret was a moody old grouch, but she certainly knew how to bake a cake.

It looked good enough to eat.

And then suddenly Horrid Henry had a horrible thought.

What if Margaret had baked a decoy cake, made with soap powder instead of flour, and left it out to tempt him to steal it? Margaret was so evil, it would be just like her to come up with such a cunning plan.

Don't let her fool you twice, screeched Henry's tummy.

He'd better take the teensiest bite, just to make sure. He'd cover up the hole with icing, no problem.

Horrid Henry took a tiny bite from the back.

Oh my.

Chocolate heaven.

This cake was great.

Wow.

But what if she'd put some bad bits in the middle? He'd better take another small bite just to check. He wouldn't want Cherry Berry to be poisoned, would he?

Chomp
Chomp
Chomp.

Horrid Henry stopped chewing.

Where had that huge hole in the cake come from? He couldn't have—

Yikes.

What was he thinking?

There was only one thing to do. He had to fill the hole fast. If he covered it with icing no one would ever know.

What could he fill the cake with to disguise the missing piece?

Newspaper?

Nah. Too bumpy.

Rice?

Too bitty.

Horrid Henry looked wildly around the kitchen.

Aha.

A sponge. A sponge for a sponge cake. He was a genius.

Quickly Horrid Henry cut the sponge to fit the hole, slipped it inside, and covered the joins with more icing.

Perfect.

No one would ever know.

Mum came into the kitchen.

'Hurry up Henry, and bring your cake out. It's street party time.'

Horrid Henry had a brilliant time at the street party. Everyone was there. Magic Martha did magic tricks in the corner. Jazzy Jim banged on his keyboard.

19

Singing Soraya warbled behind the
bouncy castle. Jolly Josh showed off his
tap dancing.

Even Margaret
playing solo
trumpet and
Perfect Peter
singing with his
band, The Golden
Goodies, couldn't
ruin Henry's mood.
He'd eyed the other
contestants as they
carried their entries
to the bake-off
table. Rude Ralph
had brought

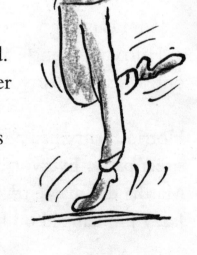

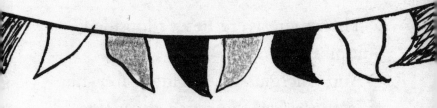

burnt brownies. Sour Susan had made horrible looking gingerbread. Greedy Graham had made a tottering tower of sweets with Chocolate Hairballs, Foam Teeth, Belcher-Squelchers and Blobby-Gobbers.

Then there were Peter's lopsided lumpies.

And Allergic Alice's gluten-free-nut-free-sugar-free-flour-free-dairy-free-beetroot-rice-cake.

Taste-free too, thought Horrid Henry.

And a rag-tag collection of droopy cakes and wobbly pies.

'Wah,' wailed Weepy William. 'I dropped mine.'

Horrid Henry and Moody Margaret shoved through the crowd as the famous judge, Cherry Berry, stood behind the cake table.

Henry had made sure his cake was at the front.

Margaret had also made sure her cake was at the front.

The two chocolate sponges faced each other.

'Nah Nah Ne Nah Nah, my cake is

best,' jeered Margaret.

'Nah Nah Ne Nah Nah, my cake is best,' jeered Henry.

They glared at each other.

Tee hee, thought Margaret.

Tee hee, thought Henry.

'Stand back from the cakes, you'll all get a chance to taste them soon,' said Cherry Berry.

She walked around the table, eyeing the goodies. She poked one, prodded another, sniffed a third. She walked around again. And again.

Then she stopped in front of Henry
and Margaret's cakes.

Henry held his breath.

Yes!

'Now, don't these sponge cakes look
lovely,' said Cherry Berry. 'So attractive.
So fluffy. Ooh, I do love a light
sponge,' she said, cutting a piece and
taking a big bite.

'So spongy,' she choked, spitting out a piece of yellow kitchen sponge. 'Ugggghhh.'

Rats, thought Horrid Henry.

Cherry Berry checked the name on the flag.

'Henry's cake is disqualified.'

Double rats, thought Horrid Henry.

'Ha ha ha ha ha,' screeched Moody Margaret.

'The winner is . . . Margaret.'

'Yes!' shrieked Margaret.

Aaaarrrggghhhhh.

That was his cake. It was so unfair. His cake had won after all. He'd pay Margaret back—

'I'll just try a little piece before we share it with everyone,' said Cherry Berry, taking a huge bite.

'Blecccchhh!' gagged Cherry, spitting it out. 'Salt! Salt instead of sugar.'

'What?' screamed Moody Margaret.

How was it possible that salt had been sneaked into her cake?

Unless . . . unless . . .

'You put a sponge in my cake,' shouted Margaret.

'You put salt in my cake,' shouted Henry.

Horrid Henry grabbed a pie and hurled it at Margaret.

Moody Margaret grabbed a cake and hurled it at Henry.

Horrid Henry ducked.

SMACK

The gooey cake landed in Cherry Berry's face.

'Food fight!' shrieked Rude Ralph, snatching cupcakes and throwing them.

26

'Food fight!' screamed Greedy
Graham, pitching pies into the crowd.

'Stop it! Stop it!' shouted Mum, as whipped cream splatted on her head.

'Stop it!' shouted Dad, as a lemon tart splatted on his shirt.

Cherry Berry brushed cake from her face and pie from her hair.

'Wah,' she wailed, as cake dripped down her back. 'I have a soggy bottom.'

She staggered over to the cake table and gripped the edge.

The table was empty except for a few grey cupcakes.

'I proclaim Peter's lopsided lumpies the winner,' she gasped.

'Yippee,' squealed Perfect Peter.

'Noooooo,' howled Horrid Henry.

2

HORRID HENRY'S CANNIBAL CURSE

It was the weekend. Yippee! No school.
No school dinners. No Miss Battle-Axe.
And best of all, no homework.

It was the weekend. Boo. Hiss. Yuck.
The weekend meant . . . chores. His
mean horrible parents weren't happy
with torturing him by sending him
to school five days a week and then
making him live with wormy worm
Peter the rest of the time.

Oh no. They had to make him suffer
as their slave as well. Did they have
any idea how much time doing chores
took? How much wonderful telly he

missed trudging up and down the stairs emptying all the waste paper baskets and cleaning out Fluffy's litter tray and putting the recycling outside?

Horrid Henry had lost hours. Months. Years of his life.

It was so unfair.

One day, one happy day, he would find a way to get out of this weekly misery. One day he would find a slave of his own who he could boss around.

Perfect Peter bounced into the sitting
room and went to the bookshelf.

'Go away,' said Horrid Henry.

'What are you doing, Henry?' asked
Peter. 'I'm going to alphabetise my
books.'

'What does it look like I'm doing,
Poopsicle?' said Henry, stretching out
on the sofa. If only he didn't have to
move.

'I'm not a poopsicle,'
said Peter.

Horrid Henry
looked at Peter the
poopsicle. And then
Horrid Henry had a
brilliant, wonderful,
spectacular idea.
Why oh why hadn't
he thought of this
before?

'It's sad you're such a baby,' said Henry.

'I am not a baby,' said Peter. 'I'm a big boy. Mum said so.'

'Do you really think you're as good as me?' said Henry. 'That anything I can do you can do?'

'Yes,' said Peter.

Of course he was as good as Henry. Better, in fact, but Perfect Peter didn't want to brag. Peter was definitely smarter. And kinder. And tidier. And he had more money in his piggy bank. And he could play the cello.

In fact the only thing Henry could do better than him was run a teensy weensy bit faster.

'I can do anything you can do,' said Peter.

'No way, Uggalina,' said Henry.

'You're a baby.'

'Am not,' said Peter. 'And don't call me Uggalina.'

'Then I dare you to run upstairs and collect all the recycling,' said Horrid Henry. 'Bet you can't do it by the time I count to twenty-five.'

'Can too,' said Peter.

'Nah,' said Henry. 'You're much too little.'

'Am not,' said Peter.

'Then prove it, baby boo boo,' said Henry. 'If you can, you'll never be a baby boo boo again.'

Perfect Peter grabbed a rubbish bag and dashed upstairs.

Horrid Henry leaned back on the sofa and counted loudly.

Tee hee.

What a brilliant way to get Peter to do his chores.

Peter dashed downstairs, gasping for breath, clutching a full bag.

'Nineteen . . . twenty . . . Peter, you did it,' said Henry. 'You're king of the rubbish.'

Perfect Peter was delighted. It wasn't often that Henry praised him.

'I knew I could do it,' said Peter, trying to stop panting. He'd never run so fast in his life.

'Wow,' said Henry. 'You really proved me wrong.'

Peter glowed. Finally, finally, Henry was recognising how clever he was. And no more being called baby boo boo.

'That was amazing,' said Henry. 'Now, let's see how fast you can clean out Fluffy's litter tray. My best time is fifty-four seconds. I'll start counting . . . now. One. Two. Thr—'

Perfect Peter raced to Fluffy's stinky

litter box by the kitchen back door.
He'd show Henry how fast he was.
Henry would never be able to call
him a nappy baby wibble pants again.

Peter grabbed the poop scoop.

Then he stopped.

A terrible thought
dribbled into his brain.

Was it possible?

Was Henry tricking
him? Tricking him
into doing his chores? Had he fallen for
Henry's tricks . . . again??

Perfect Peter smelled a rat.

No. No. NOOOOOOO!

'Mum,' wailed Peter. 'Henry tricked
me into doing his chores.'

Uh oh, thought Henry.

'Don't be horrid, Henry,' shouted
Mum. 'Do your own chores or no TV
for a week.'

'I don't know what you're talking about,' bellowed Henry. 'We were just having a race.'

Perfect Peter came back into the room. He wanted to pour cat litter all over Henry, and kick the recycling bag.

'Do it,' said his devil. 'Live for once.'

'Don't do it,' said his angel. 'Then you'd be horrid too.'

Eeeeeek.

'Tell-tale,' hissed Henry.

'Serves you right, Henry,' said Peter. How could he have thought Henry was being nice to him for once? He swore he'd never fall for one of Henry's tricks ever ever again.

Peter glared at Henry.

Henry smiled at Peter.

'I've written a song for you, Peter,' said Horrid Henry.

He jumped on the sofa and began to sing:

'Oh I'm a big fat ninny
A skinny minny ninny
I'm a strudel-noodle tart
And all I do is far—'

'Mum,' screamed Peter. 'Henry called me a ninny. And a strudel-noodle.'

39

'Did not,' said Horrid Henry. 'I was just singing a song.'

'That's it, Henry,' said Mum, running into the room. 'No pocket money for a week.'

No pocket money? And all because of his wormy worm brother?

'But I wasn't doing anything,' howled Henry. 'Is it a crime to sing a song in this house?'

Ding Dong.

It was Rude Ralph come over to play. He was holding a lumpy plastic bag.

They went up to Henry's bedroom.

'No worms allowed,' said Henry, slamming the door. He had to pay Peter back for getting him into trouble for singing. It was so unfair.

'What's in the bag?' said Horrid Henry.

40

'Shrunken heads,' said Rude Ralph.

'Ooh,' said Henry.

Ralph pulled two hideous skull heads from the bag. They had big empty eye sockets, and scary wisps of long straggly blonde and brown hair. They looked— they looked absolutely marvellous.

'Wow,' said Henry. 'Wow.' He reached out and touched the gruesome skulls.

He wanted those heads more than anything in the world.

'Where'd you get them?'

'Present from my gran,' said Ralph. 'These two are for you.'

'Thanks, Ralph,' said Henry.

Did anyone ever have a better friend than Ralph?

'This one looks like Margaret,' said Horrid Henry, swinging one of the heads by its pony tail.

'Just better-looking,' said Ralph rudely.

Henry and Ralph hung up the heads from the ceiling light. Yeah! The heads looked really horrible. Horrid Henry shivered.

Ralph grabbed hold of Henry's metal headband from his Evil Scientist Robot Kit and shoved it on top of his hair.

'Oooh, aaaahhh, eeeee, my head is

shrinking . . .' yelped Ralph, writhing in his chair and laughing.

Horrid Henry stared at Ralph. He'd just had the most brilliant idea ever in the history of the universe.

If he could make Peter believe he could shrink heads, Peter would be in his power. He could make Peter give him all his crisps. He could get Peter's pocket money. He'd never have to steal Peter's chips again . . . Peter would just hand them over . . . or else. He would rule the house as King Henry the Horrible . . . forever.

'Peter!' bellowed Henry. 'Come quick. I have a present for you.'

Perfect Peter poked his head round the door.

'What?' said Peter.

'Who do you want?' asked Henry. 'Margaret or Susan?'

Huh?

'Up there,' said Horrid Henry, pointing.

Perfect Peter stared at the skulls dangling from the ceiling lamp. One had a dark pony tail. The other had a few blonde tufts.

'What are they?' said Peter cautiously.

'Margaret and Susan,' said
Horrid Henry. 'They've
annoyed me for the very last
time. I shrank their heads.'

'Shame you missed it,'
said Ralph.

Perfect Peter stared up at
the shrunken heads.

No way. Absolutely no
way.

'I don't believe you,' said Peter. He
took a step back.

'I know an ancient cannibal curse,'
said Henry. 'From my top secret curse
book. When I say the curse, with the
help of my trusty head-shrinker—pow!'

Perfect Peter recoiled.

He knew Henry was lying.

Henry had to be lying.

Henry couldn't really shrink heads . . .
could he?

45

'You're lying,' said Peter.

'I'll prove it,' said Henry. 'If you're so
sure I'm lying, then put on the head-
shrinker and we'll find out.' He held up
the metal headband. 'All you have to
lose is your head.'

'NOOO!' said Peter.

'Why not?' said Horrid Henry.
'You'll be famous. You'll be helping
science. I can't believe
you don't want to take
part in this experiment.
You'll change history,
Peter. Headless statues
will be raised to you
everywhere.'

Oooh, thought
Peter. A
headless statue
of me. Wait
a minute . . .

'I don't want to be a shrunken head,' said Peter. He edged away towards the door.

Rude Ralph stepped forward.

'I'll volunteer,' he said.

'Are you sure?' said Henry.

'Yes,' said Ralph. 'You need proof of your great invention. Just . . . just call it, The Ralph.'

'I promise,' said Horrid Henry. 'Thank you, Ralph. It's been great knowing you.'

Henry placed the metal shrinker over Ralph's head.

Perfect Peter watched, horrified, as Henry slowly tightened the screws.

'And now I will begin the head-shrink curse,' said Horrid Henry. He bowed his head and raised his arms to the ceiling.

'Oh, mighty head-shrinkers from the past,

Oonga Noonu and Aladocious Mimocious

Gather round and have a blast . . .'

Rude Ralph began to shudder and shake. Henry carried on.

'You have your flesh, oh Oonga
You have your power, oh Aladocious
You have your magic, oh spirits.
Take this head, squeeze it tight
Kooka boo kooka boo kooka boo—'
Rude Ralph gave a blood-curdling scream.

Perfect Peter yelped and ran out of the room.

'Mum! Help!!' wailed Peter, running downstairs. 'Henry is shrinking Ralph's head!'

Henry and Ralph choked with laughter.

'Henry. Get down here this minute,' shouted Mum. 'You horrid boy.'

Horrid Henry rolled his eyes.

'I'll be right back,' he said to Ralph, heading downstairs.

'Henry said he'd shrunk Margaret and Susan's heads,' whimpered Peter.

'And now he's shrinking Ralph's . . .'

'Henry, that was a horrible trick to play on Peter,' said Mum.

'It wasn't a trick,' said Henry. 'I was just doing a science experiment.'

'Henry, why can't you play nicely with your brother?' said Mum.

'I was playing nicely,' said Henry. 'I even offered to give Peter one of my shrunken heads as a present.'

And then Horrid Henry heard a piercing voice coming from next door's garden.

'It's hard being the most popular girl in the class. Everyone wants to be my friend,' brayed Moody Margaret.

'You aren't the most popular girl,' yelled Susan sourly. 'Everyone thinks you're a mean old bossy boots.'

Perfect Peter gasped.

'You said you'd shrunk their heads,' he said. 'You lied.'

'I did shrink their heads,' said Henry. 'And then I unshrunk them.'

Mum sighed.

'Henry, I want you to leave Peter alone.'

Horrid Henry stared at his feet.

'Yes, Mum.'

Tra la la.

He'd got off lightly, thanks to his weasel words.

Henry dashed back upstairs and burst into his bedroom.

51

'Ralph! I got away with it. No
punishment for me.'

Horrid Henry looked around.

No Ralph.

'Ralph?' said Henry.

On the chair where Ralph had been
sitting was the headshrinker.

Inside the shrinker was . . .
a shrunken head.

Ralph had
vanished.

'Ralph?' said
Henry.

That was odd.

'Ralph? You in the loo?'

Henry looked. No Ralph.

He checked under his bed.

No Ralph.

Slowly Horrid Henry approached the
chair.

The skull had brown hair. Just like

Ralph's.

'Ralph! Stop fooling around,' said Horrid Henry.

His heart began to pound.

Was Ralph—gone?

What had he done? What would he do?

'Nah na na nah nah,' yelped Ralph, leaping out of the wardrobe. 'Tricked you!'

AAAAAAARRRRGGGG-HHHHHHH!

3

....

HORRiD HENRY'S EXTRA HORRiD GUIDE TO PERFECT PARENTS

Shhh. Shhh.

Are you alone? Is anyone watching you read this? Spies are everywhere. Find a private place where your parents and brothers and sisters can't see you . . .

Okay good. Then I'll begin.

My first guide to Perfect Parents was too popular. And too dangerous. Parents bought all the copies and hid them. They knew once my Purple Hand Gang got hold of my Top Tips for parent control they'd never be the boss again.

But I couldn't let all that fantastic, amazing advice go to waste.

So.

Here's my plan.

Inside this book I've copied down all the best bits from my Parent Taming manual. And then I've added even more fantastic advice.

Study my extra horrid guide and perfect parents can be yours. My top tips will teach you everything you need to know about training your parents. After all, who's the boss? You? Or them?

Too right, you. And don't let them forget it. It's hard, heavy work training perfect parents, but do it right and it will be worth it.

Remember, hide this book from prying eyes, including tell-tale little brothers and sisters. It's your secret weapon.

And oh yeah. I know you'll thank me forever, but words are cheap. All donations gratefully received.

Perfect Parents

Perfect parents let you do whatever you want, whenever you want. They let you decide what's for dinner, never make you eat vegetables, and give you control of the TV remote. They always blame your brothers and sisters whenever there's a quarrel. But how, I hear you scream, can you turn your mean, horrible, bossy parents into perfect ones? Just follow my simple training tips. It's all about Discipline, Rewards, Consistency, and Limits.

Shame and Tame

Remind your parents daily how
marvellous your friends' parents
are. Sigh loudly and
say, 'I wish I had
Ralph's parents.
They always let
him stay up late/eat
as many sweets as he
wants/watch loads
of TV etc.' Other
great phrases
to shame and tame parents:
'Margaret's parents gave her
a Demon Dagger Sabre';
'Josh's parents let him pour
his own chocolate
sauce'; 'Gurinder's
parents give loads
more pocket money

than you'; 'Susan's parents let her play on the computer for as long as she likes.'

Telling them how wonderful other parents are will make them want to shape up fast.

make parents feel guilty

Believe it or not, most parents try their best. Shame their best is so bad. But that's why it's a cinch to make your parents feel guilty.

Try using any of the phrases below. Once you make them feel guilty, then give them a chance to feel better by giving you what you want.

'You must feel terrible being such a bad parent.'

'Ralph's mum is much nicer than you.'

'Everyone else gets more pocket money than I do.'

'Margaret doesn't have a sweet day.'

'You're the worst Dad in the world and I hate you.'

Note. The last phrase is a bit extreme and only for use in dire emergencies.

Praise good behaviour

No one likes being told off all the time. Even parents. So remember gang, when they give you those extra sweets you deserve, or let you watch extra TV, PRAISE their good behaviour. You want to make them do this all the time. Parents want praise and attention, so give it to them. Trust me, they'll be rushing to stuff extra desserts into you, and letting you off your chores. Speaking of chores . . .

How to make your parents do your chores for_you

 What are you, a slave? How dare parents ask you to help around the house. Don't you have enough to do as it is?

Have you ever heard that phrase, 'If you want

something done well, do it yourself?'
Parents know this is true, so your goal is
to do all chores so slowly, and so badly,
and so ungraciously, and with so much
wailing and gnashing and groaning and
moaning and sighing, that your parents
will give up and yell: 'Oh, all right, I'll
do it myself.'

Victory!

Congratulations. You are now well
on your way to having perfectly trained
parents.

Tantrums

All parents have tantrums. They yell and
scream when they don't get their way
(ie. when you don't do what they want).
Just remember, you'd have tantrums too
if you were old and wrinkly like them.
My advice is, keep cool. Suggest your

parent has a time-out. If you are really an expert parent tamer, urge them to sit on the naughty step until they calm down.

Of course, tantrums are *your* secret weapon.

Tantrums are best staged in public, or just before your parents have to go somewhere important, or when guests are over. Believe me they'll promise you anything if you'll only just STOP screaming.

Best Tantrum Positions

Face down on the floor is best. This means you can kick and squeal, and

make lots of extra noise.
Plus, if you are fake
crying, it's much
easier to do this
when your parents
can only *hear* and
not see you.

Money

You want it. They have it. It's
so unfair. Why do parents
have so much more
money than you do?
Wouldn't it be great if
you could have all
the cash, and give
them pocket money?
Well, when I'm
King that's exactly
what will happen.

Till then, you just have to try and get as much money as you can by making your parents feel guilty.

Tell them everyone gets loads more pocket money than you do.

Remind them of all the things you need to buy.

Point out that they can't expect any presents from you if they give you so little money.

Tell them you need to practice money management skills and you can't on the pitiful amount they give you.

If all else fails . . . tell them it's time for a raise.

Sadly, there are always things that you want that for some reason parents don't want you to have. For example, Roller Bowlers, the world's best trainers, the shoes on wheels you  can set to Screech; Fire-engine; Drums; Cannon; Siren; and Sonic Boom. They're so loud you can hear them from miles off! Wow! So, how do you make them buy you great stuff like that? You BORE and NAG them to death. Just go on and on and on about them. Believe me they will eventually give in just to keep you quiet. Then don't forget, PRAISE GOOD BEHAVIOUR. You want to reinforce this excellent conduct and help your parents make good choices.

That way, next time you won't have to whine quite so much.

How to get the food you want

Just one word—allergies. I know I'm allergic to fruit, vegetables, soup, salad, and muesli. In fact, the only food I can eat is chocolate, cake, crisps, burgers, pizza and sweets.

How to get your siblings into trouble

Why should you take the rap? Divert your parents' attention onto the guilty—your annoying brothers and sisters. Remember. You're always right. They're always wrong.

Unfortunately, parents don't always see things clearly. They might blame you, even though it's never your fault.

Here's how to train your parents to see things your way.

Make sure you start yelling first. Don't wait to be accused of stealing your brother's chips. Loudly accuse him of stealing/hitting/pinching/teasing etc.

'He/she started it,' is your go-to phrase.

But remember.

There's one skill you MUST learn. Crying on command. Whatever happens, your parents must find YOU in tears. Trust me, screeching 'He hit me,' or 'She pinched me,' while wailing and gnashing and gulping and sobbing will carry so much more weight, even if (gasp) you were the one who started the fight.

Your younger brothers and sisters already know this fact. That's why they use pretend crying all the time.

Just because you're older, don't forget this invaluable tip.

When in doubt – CRY.

When you're in the wrong – CRY.

When you've teased them – CRY.

Get your tears in first.

Weasel Words

Remember my favourite charity, Child in Need? The one I collect money for?

That's a perfect example of weasel words. I'm a child. I'm in need. 100% totally true. Can I help it if whoever gives me money gets the wrong idea?

Tee hee.

Weasel words can come to your rescue in tight spots.

'I didn't touch his sweets.' (I *ate* them)

'Dad said I could.' (Well, he did—once.)

'Peter hit me!' (He did, once, when he was a baby. I didn't say *when* he did . . .)

'I've only watched an hour of TV.' (The TV was on for hours but I wasn't watching it.)

When all else fails, deny everything. You have no idea how those biscuits ended up in your room.

TV

Remember the
magic word? No,
it's not please,
it's homework.
You'd be amazed
how much TV
you can watch
by saying it's for

homework. Parents like to feel they're
helping their children in school, so
what better way to help than to let kids
watch 'educational' programmes like
Terminator Gladiator, Mutant Max, and
Hog House (tee hee).

Bedtime

Always tricky. Parents want you in bed
as early as possible. You, of course, want

to stay up as late as possible. So if your bedtime is 8 o'clock, here are some parent-training tips to get that extra time you deserve. One is sure to work.

1. Tell them everyone gets to stay up later than you do.

2. Delay bedtime for as long as possible. See how slowly you can brush your teeth. Drag your feet as you stagger up the stairs to your bedroom. Take hours putting on your pyjamas. Say you need to do your homework. Ask for endless drinks of water. Once in bed, keep coming downstairs. Any excuse will do.

3. Once you have tormented them sufficiently, promise that if they let you stay up an hour later, you'll go to bed

with no fuss. (Then keep your word, and your parents will learn that they can spend an hour struggling to heave you into bed at 8 o'clock, or have a quiet evening with no fuss and stress and argument. The well-trained parent will make the right choice.)

Congratulations

Well done! You are
now the proud owner
of perfectly trained
and tamed parents.
You call the shots, as
you lounge around
eating chocolates and
guzzling Fizzywizz
drinks while your
perfect parents wait

on you hand and foot, eager to do whatever—

Wait, what's that you're saying? You did everything I told you, and they aren't tamed? Then they must have read this book, and armed themselves against all your weasel words. I did warn you, this information is top-secret, how could you let your parents get hold of

this book, now they'll know exactly
how to—

Come to think of it, I wonder if that's
why my parents seem to be resisting
their training . . .

Oops.

4

HORRID HENRY'S
BAD BOOK

'Henry. Get down here.'

'Henry. We're waiting for you.'

'I'm READING!' bellowed Horrid
Henry.

How could he go out with his mean,
horrible parents before he found out
what Evil Evie would do next?

Evil Evie came up with the best tricks.
The time she pretended to be allergic
to vegetables! Or put slugs in her sister's
slippers for April Fools! Or swapped her
parents. Or saved the planet by refusing
to take baths. Or won the lottery

and spent every penny on toys and chocolate. Or rode in the car with a pot of lasagne on her lap and accidentally took the lid off . . .

Wow.

Why couldn't he have a brilliant sister like Evie instead of a waste of space wormy toad brother like Peter?

'Not those awful books *again*,' said Dad.

'Can't you find anything better to
read?' said Mum.

'These are the best books ever,' said
Horrid Henry.

'Too mean,' said Mum.

'Too aggressive,' said Dad.

Horrid Henry sighed.

First, his parents complained that
he only read comics. Then, after he'd
discovered the best books ever in the
history of the universe and couldn't stop
reading them over and over and over
again, and even bought them with his
own precious pocket money, his parents
complained that they hated the Evil
Evie series.

'Such a bad example,' said Mum.

'They put ideas into his head,' said Dad.

'Why can't you read books about
good children who always obey their
parents?' they moaned.

Horrid Henry rolled his eyes. Wasn't reading meant to be about fun and adventure and escape? He got enough real life in real life.

Horrid Henry loved Evil Evie.

Rude Ralph loved Evil Evie.

Moody Margaret loved Evil Evie.

In fact, everyone at school loved Evil Evie.

Even Miss Battle-Axe loved the Evil Evie books and read her adventures out loud every day during story-time.

Evil Evie and the Roaring Rogues. Evil Evie and the Tyrant Teacher. Evil Evie and the Mad Scientist. Evil Evie, Pirate Queen.

They were definitely the funniest books ever.

Horrid Henry could win any Evil Evie competition. He knew everything about her.

Her favourite vegetable: ketchup.

83

Her catch-phrase: Buzz off, banana-head.

Her favourite word: swashbuckling.

Her favourite colour: purple (just like his).

Her favourite TV programme: Robot Riot.

Her evilest enemies: Rotten Robert, the monster next door, and Snobby Bobby, her stuck-up cousin.

Her secret job: Spy Assassin.

Her foul sister: Wilting Willa, an infant fiend in training.

Her pet rat: Doris.

Her hometown: Rudeville.

Her mean, horrible parents. Hmmm, they didn't appear to have names. Probably because they were so old they'd forgotten them, thought Horrid Henry.

Evil Evie was Horrid Henry's Mastermind subject.

Best of all, every time Henry got into
trouble, he blamed Evil Evie.

'Evie did that,' he squealed when
Mum told him off for poking Peter.

'Evie did that,' he shrieked when Dad
told him off for calling Peter names.

'Evie did that,' lied Henry, when
Mum and Dad told him off for calling
the police when Miss Battle-Axe refused
to give him sweets.

After all, his parents hadn't read the Evil Evie books, had they? How would they know?

Tee hee.

'Mum!' squealed Peter. 'Henry called me wimpadoodle and wibble wobble pants.'

'Stop being horrid, Henry,' said Mum.

'Henry was never horrid until he started reading those horrible books,' said Dad.

'Those books are a bad influence,' said Mum. 'He always played nicely with Peter before.'

'Really?' said Grandma. 'I don't remember that.'

From next door came the sound of slapping.

'I hate you, Susan,' screamed Margaret.

'I hate you more,' screamed Susan.

Moody Margaret's mum leaned over the garden wall.

'You know how my little Maggie Moo Moo has always been the sweetest, kindest, quietest child ever,' said her mother. 'A jewel. Perfect in every way. Well, ever since she discovered Evil Evie she's become . . . a total terror.'

'Henry too,' said Mum. 'I'm sure he'd play beautifully with his brother if those books hadn't put ideas into his head.'

'I'm sick and tired of these terrible

books,' said Margaret's mother. 'Margaret's become so moody since she started reading them.'

Horrid Henry looked up from his book, *Evil Evie Stings the Scorpion*.

'Margaret's been a moody old grouch since she was a tadpole,' said Henry.

'Don't be horrid, Henry,' said Mum.

'I never read Evil Evie,' said Peter. 'I'd much rather read about good children.'

'Quite right, Peter,' said Mum.

Horrid Henry pounced.

He was a giant mosquito dive-bombing for his supper.

'Aiieeeeee!' squealed Peter. 'Henry pinched me.'

'Evil Evie did that to her sister,' said Horrid Henry. 'I was just copying her.'

Tee hee. Evil Evie was the best get out of jail free card ever.

Horrid Henry walked into his bedroom after a long day at school.

Phew.

Finally, a chance to relax on his bed with a favourite Evil Evie, maybe *Evil Evie and the Dastardly Demon—*

Huh?

His special Evil Evie bookcase was empty.

'Where are my Evil Evie books?' shrieked Henry. 'Someone's stolen them.'

'Banned,' said Mum, coming into the room.

'Banned,' said Dad. 'We're sick
and tired of your horrid copy-cat
behaviour.'

Oops.

Horrid Henry hadn't thought of that.
He thought he'd been brilliant blaming
everything on Evie. And now his
brilliance had backfired.

'But I want to read,' wailed Horrid
Henry.

'And that's why we've got a present for you, Henry,' said Mum. 'The fabulous Gallant Gary series. Much better than Evil Evie. Margaret's mum recommended them.'

She handed Henry a book with a sparkling silver cover. There was a picture of a boy holding a tea towel, with a halo framing his brown curls.

'Gallant . . . Gary?' said Horrid Henry.
He read the story titles:

Blecccccchhh.

Horrid Henry opened the book as if it were radioactive and flicked through the grisly pages.

There was Gallant Gary helping an old lady across the street.

There was Gallant Gary telling his Mum to rest her feet while he cleared the table and did loads of chores.

There was Gallant Gary playing catch with his adorable younger brother Little Larry.

Blecccccchhh.

Horrid Henry slammed the book shut. Ugggh.

Didn't he have enough goody goodies in his life with Peter?

'These stories are boring,' said Henry. 'I want my Evil Evie books back.'

'Maybe you'll learn something,' said Mum.

'Maybe you'll stop being so horrid,' said Dad.

'Why don't you copy Gary?' said Mum. 'That would be wonderful.'

'NO!' screamed Henry.

At lunchtime Horrid Henry went to his school library. Why hadn't he thought of this before? Tra la la, he'd check out some Evil Evie books and cover them with Gallant Gary covers. Tra la la, a trick worthy of Evie herself . . .

What?

The Evil Evie shelf was empty.

'All the Evil Evie books are checked out, I'm afraid,' said the librarian, Beaming Bea. 'I have lots of Gallant Gary if you want to try something new.'

'NOOOOOOO,' said Horrid Henry. 'I want to read Evil Evie!!'

'You and everyone else,' said the librarian.

He had to get his books back. He had to. He couldn't get to sleep without an Evil Evie book. He couldn't relax after school without an Evil Evie book.

Why had he ever blamed Evie for being horrid? What would Evie do in this dreadful situation?

And then suddenly Horrid Henry had a brilliant, spectacular idea. It was so brilliant, and so spectacular, that Henry started dancing around the library, whooping and cheering.

'Shhh,' said Beaming Bea, frowning.

What was it Mum had said? Why
didn't he copy Gary?

Copy Gallant Gary, thought Henry.
Copy Gallant Gary. Boy could he copy
Gallant Gary.

On their way to the park Horrid Henry
grabbed Grandma and tugged on her
arm.

'I'm helping you cross the road,' he shouted.

'But I don't want to cross the road,' said Grandma.

'Too bad,' said Henry, yanking her. 'You're an old lady and you're crossing.'

'Help!' squealed Grandma.

'Henry stop that at once,' shouted Mum.

Henry stopped. 'But I'm only copying Gary, like you said. He's always helping old ladies cross the road.'

Mum opened her mouth and then closed it.

SQUELCH
SQUERCH.

'Mum!' squealed Peter.

Mum ran into the sitting room. Great globs of soapy suds bubbled from the carpet up to Peter's knees.

'What's going on?' said Mum. 'Henry! What have you done?' she said, looking at the bubbling carpet.

'I was just copying Gary,' said Henry, squirting more shampoo. 'I know you wanted to shampoo the carpet and I was trying to help you with your chores just like Gary.'

'Stop,' said Mum, as her feet sank in the suds. 'Uhhm, thank you Henry, that's enough.'

That night, after supper, Horrid Henry leapt to his feet.

'I'll clear,' said Horrid Henry,
gathering all the dirty plates and heading
towards the kitchen.

CRASH
SMASH

Broken plates cascaded round the
floor.

'Henry!' shouted Dad.

'I'm copying Gary, just like you said,'
said Henry. 'He always clears the table.'

'Oh,' said Mum.

'Oh,' said Dad.

'C'mon Peter, let's play catch in the
garden,' said Horrid Henry.

Perfect Peter stared. Henry never offered to play with him.

Mum smiled. 'Yes, go on Peter,' she said.

'Just like Gallant Gary and Little Larry,' said Henry, hurling the ball.

The ball torpedoed through the kitchen window.

CRASH.

Glass splinters flew everywhere as the window shattered.

'HENRY!' screamed Mum and Dad.

'I'm so sorry,' said Horrid Henry.

'I was just copying Gary. He and Little Larry are always playing catch.'

Mum looked at Dad.

Dad looked at Mum.

They stared at the broken window,
the soapy carpet and the smashed dishes.

'Don't worry,' said Horrid Henry. 'I'll
keep copying Gary, just like you said.'

'Oh,' said Mum.

'Oh,' said Dad.

Horrid Henry came home from school the next day and walked slowly up to his bedroom. No TV. No chance to relax with an Evil Evie book—

Henry stared. His special bookshelf was full. Packed to the brim with Evil Evie books.

Evil Evie was back. Gallant Gary was gone.

Yippee!!!!!!

Horrid Henry picked up his favourite book and lay back on his bed.

He turned to the first page and began to read.

Evie was Evil.

Everyone said so, even her mother.

ALARA A KAYANI

14·11·2019 .